As de Old People

Would Say

A Collection of Caribbean Pearls of Wisdom & Expressions

DESIREE FOY-FISHER

Acknowledgements

Thank you to everyone that responded to the numerous phone calls and emails over the years and met with me to share the proverbs & expressions that have meant the most to you. And THANK YOU to those that kept me motivated and encouraged to follow this through. Lastly, thank you to the historians whose mission is to never let us forget.

Extra Special Thanks To

David & Cassandra Foy, Michael Fisher, Jr.; Darren Foy, Luz Smith-Allick, Idalia Bess, Simone Bess, Darwin Foy, Charles Fahie, Gerry Thomas, Rosalie Torres, Michael Fisher, Sr.; Daniel Fisher, Timothy Fisher, Gwyneth Hendricks, Kimbra Danet, Grace Kisa, Maurice Evans, Audene Watson, Lizette Llanos Popo, Jessica Rosado, Mike Williams, Joan Cook, Marilyn Krigger and Kris Richards.

Photo Credits

Michael Fisher, Jr.; Michael Fisher, Sr.; Daniel Fisher, Desiree Foy-Fisher and stock.thelifedesignagency.com
Island wildlife candids were taken at Coral World Ocean Park on St. Thomas, USVI
Cover Image: Portland, Jamaica

ISBN-13: 978-1-4507-3332-8
Copyright © 2013 by WordLick Media
Printed in China

Design: CREATIVE. The Life Design Agency

Contact

WordLick Media
P.O. Box 4767
Alpharetta, Georgia 30023
www.wordlickmedia.com

Dedicated to

Rosita Frett, *my inspiration.*

David & Cassandra Foy, *my strength.*

HANS LOLLIK & LITTLE HANS LOLLIK, USVI

NOBODY WANT TO FIX DE WELL UNTIL SOMEBODY CHILE FALL IN

Be proactive, not reactive.

Wen yoh know betta, do betta.

When you know better, do better.

Who doan hear does feel.

When you don't follow instructions or heed advice,
you'll learn the hard way.

Once a man, Twice a chile.

We are only adults once in our lives and
are like children in the beginning and end.

VIRGIN GORDA, BVI

De devil
is a
busy man.

The Devil's been keeping you busy.

Goat doan bring sheep.

Your child is a reflection of you.

THE BATHS, VIRGIN GORDA, BVI

Yoh pissin' on ah hot rock and smellin' it.

When a young man starts to act like a man
without the maturity to be one.

An' dat is plain English speakin'!

Needing no explanation.

MONGOOSE GOT NO BUSINESS IN DE FOWL HOUSE.

Describing someone in a position that they can exploit.

THE BATHS, VIRGIN GORDA, BVI

De remedy to fall is 'Get up'.

The cure for a fall is to get back on your feet.

Ev'ry skin teet' is not a smile.

Every smile does not come with good intentions.

LEAVE
"Should ah known"
ALONE.

Don't put yourself in a situation to regret the outcome and later say, "If I had known..." or "I should have known..."

I AIN' MAKIN' NO JOKIN'!

I'm serious.

De cheapest does come de dearest.

Being frugal and cutting corners may
cost you more in the end.

Quiet dawg does bite hawd.

Do not underestimate a person with a quiet demeanor.

33

See an' doan see.

See no evil...

YOH GOT IT LIKE A WEDDIN', CALLIN' IT A B*TCH OF A SPREE!

Life is good and you have no idea how good
you've got it – quit complaining.

THE BATHS, VIRGIN GORDA, BVI

If yoh han' writin
look like chicken scratch,
doan blame de pen.

Take responsibility for your actions.

LITTLE DIX BAY, VIRGIN GORDA, BVI

De lazy do tings twice.

Do it right the first time.

KEY WEST, FLORIDA

Ah come
yoh ah come.

You'll be where I am in time.

Jig de bottom,
Look de top.

Be thorough.

You givin' me a 6 for a 9.

You're trying to deceive me.

De first ratta get in, haul in he tail.

Secure what you have or someone else will take it.

WEN YO SMELL YO NE'BA POT BUNNIN', PUT WATTA IN YOURS.

Don't worry about your neighbor's troubles,
make sure your household is in order.
Learn from other's mistakes.

51

Doan hang yoh hat whe yoh han' cyan reach.

Don't overextend yourself.

Betta belly bus' dan good vittles spoil.

Better to have a full stomach than
to let good food go to waste.

Wen yoh give away yoh *sshole, yo have to sh*t tru yoh ribs.

Sometimes helping others can backfire.

Yoh lookin for me,
an wen yoh
fine me,
yoh gon fine out.

Provoke me and deal with the consequences.

Who bring does carry.

Those that bring gossip to you will gossip about you.

THE BATHS, VIRGIN GORDA, BVI

TELL DE DEVIL YOH AIN'T FINE ME!

Don't bring trouble my way.

Today fo me.
Tomorrow fo you.

Your day is coming.

Yoh cyan catch a fish unless he open he mout.

You got yourself in trouble.

soursop
doan fall far
from de tree.

Your child is a reflection of you.

BLUE LAGOON, PORT ANTONIO, JAMAICA

Bull horn not too heavy fo he carry.

Everyone must carry his own load.

Mongst yoh sex!

Know your place.

KEY WEST, FLORIDA

Wen you was comin, I was goin.

The circle of life.

YOH EYES BIGGA DAN YOH STOMACH

You thought you could eat more than
your stomach could hold.

KEY WEST, FLORIDA, USA

Shut yoh door an' lick yoh chile.

Take care of your personal business in private.

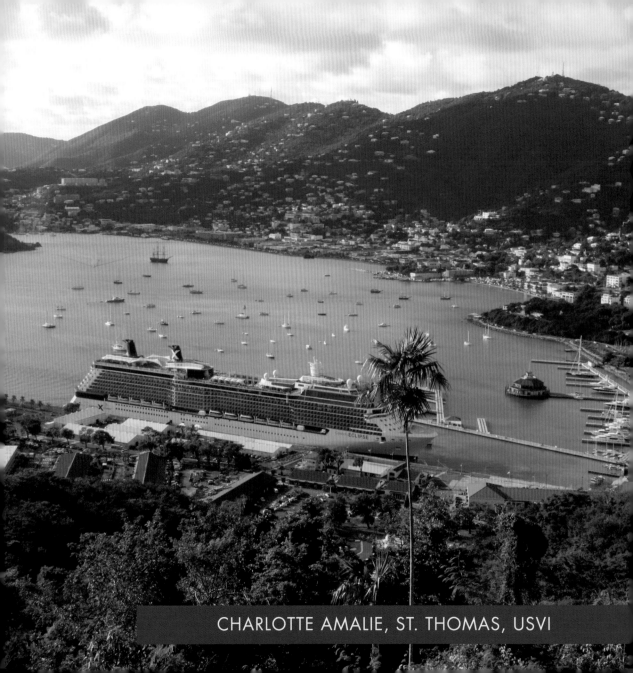

CHARLOTTE AMALIE, ST. THOMAS, USVI

Doan spoil yoh self!

Quit while you're ahead.

WATER & HASSEL ISLAND, USVI

Wat yoh do in de dark will come out in de light.

Eventually the truth will be told.

_____

WHISTLING CAY, USVI

YOH HAUNTED?

Asked when someone's actions are restless and mischievous.

Yoh ears must be unda yoh foot!

It's the only explanation for why you're not listening.

STOP HARBORIN' DEM †ING!

Don't keep pests and nuisances around.
Stop holding onto those ill feelings—let it go.

THE BATHS, VIRGIN GORDA, BVI

YOH HEAD HAWD LIKE ROCK STONE.

Describing someone that's the worst kind of stubborn.

BLUEFIELDS, WESTMORELAND, JAMAICA

WHAT DOAN KILL WILL FATTEN!

What doesn't kill you makes you stronger.

STAY OUT AH BIG PEOPLE BUSINESS

Stay out of adult affairs. Mind your own business.

well now
yoh look
like people!

It's a compliment given when you look
polished and presentable.

ST. JOHN, USVI

LOOK
DE KETTLE
CALLIN' DE POT

BLACK!

How are you going to talk about me
when you're in the same situation I am in.

Bite an' Swallow.

Take a moment to process. Accept it. Move on.

_____

TRUNK BAY, ST. JOHN, USVI

go
wash
yoh
daylight

Particularly for women...take care of your girlie parts.

Watta boilin' an' fish doan know.

Said when someone is plotting and scheming against someone else and they have no idea.

VIRGIN GORDA, BVI

Get from behind God back.

Stop trying to do your dirt where you think no one is seeing you.

WHEN YOH DIGGIN A HOLE, DIG TWO.

What you plan for someone else may backfire,
so prepare for your own downfall.

Chew yoh tobacco, be careful whe yoh spit.

Have your fun but be careful about
with whom and how you do it.

She'
comin' to come.

Making others proud by doing what you do well.
Coming into your own.